Aurora's Royal Wedding

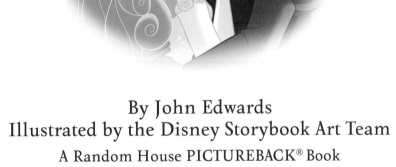

By John Edwards
Illustrated by the Disney Storybook Art Team
A Random House PICTUREBACK® Book

Random House 🏠 New York

randomhouse.com/kids
ISBN 978-0-7364-3167-5
MANUFACTURED IN CHINA
10 9 8 7 6 5 4 3 2 1

Princess Aurora had a lot to be grateful for. She was no longer a sleeping beauty, thanks to Prince Phillip and the three good fairies. Maleficent was long gone, and Aurora was back with her mother and father. And best of all, she and Phillip had found true love.

Even though their parents had decided years earlier that Phillip and Aurora would marry, Phillip wanted to make a proper proposal. He kneeled and asked Aurora to be his wife. Of course Aurora said yes!

The Queen celebrated her daughter's good news with a cup of tea. "I couldn't be more delighted to have my daughter home," she said, "but I'll leave you now so you can make all the royal decisions regarding the wedding."

"Thank you, Mother," said Aurora. The princess was excited but nervous. This would be her first job as a princess.

As soon as the Queen exited the room, the dressmakers
burst in with gowns of many colors and styles. "They're all
so lovely, how will I ever choose?" asked Aurora.

When Aurora tried to select the table settings for the reception, she became even more confused. "Maybe I'm not ready to be a princess," she said to Merryweather.

"Nonsense," replied the good fairy. "You'll make the finest princess this kingdom has ever seen."

Still, Aurora was worried.

Just then, Prince Phillip came by and suggested they go for a walk. "I'm not sure how to act like a princess," Aurora told him. "I can't even choose a dress!"

Phillip looked at her sweetly. "My dear, you will be a wonderful princess. But if you're worried, I think I know someone who can help," he said.

Back at the palace, Flora, Fauna, and Merryweather were trying to come up with a plan to help Aurora. "Let's use our wands!" said Flora.

"Magic won't help," Merryweather grumbled. "Aurora needs to feel like a princess on the inside."

"We should ask the Queen!" Fauna declared.

Prince Phillip had the same idea as the good fairies. He sent the Queen to Aurora's room. "I understand you are worried," the Queen told her daughter, "but being a princess isn't about what you do. Rather, it's about who you are. A princess is honest, compassionate, intelligent, and kind. And you, my dear, are all those things."

"Oh, thank you, Mother!" Aurora cried. "I have an idea about my wedding gown. Would it be possible to wear yours?"

The Queen smiled. "I married your father in a simple but beautiful gown. I think it will fit you perfectly."

The day of the royal wedding finally arrived. Prince Phillip smiled as King Stefan walked Aurora down the aisle. She looked every bit a princess in her mother's gown—and she was starting to feel like one, too.

"Do you, Prince Phillip, take Princess
Aurora as your wife?"
"I do!"

"Do you, Princess Aurora, take Prince
Phillip as your husband?"
"I do!"

After the ceremony, the royal couple greeted their guests at the reception. Everyone enjoyed a lovely meal. And the prince and princess shared a piece of the magnificent wedding cake.

Then it was time for their first dance. Surrounded by their parents and good friends, Phillip and Aurora happily twirled across the dance floor. The Queen was very proud of her daughter. She had grown into a lovely young lady and a true princess!

As Phillip and Aurora rode off in the royal carriage, they looked forward to a wonderful future together as prince and princess.

Eric and Ariel smiled. They knew
they'd had the best wedding day
anyone could ever ask for. It was
the beginning of a life filled with
joy and laughter—and family
and friends from the land
and the sea.

The vows were read. The rings were exchanged.
"Kiss the girl!" cried Sebastian.
And at last, the prince and princess were married!

The wedding day finally arrived. The human guests sat on the deck of the ship, while the merfolk watched from the sea. King Triton used his magic trident to lift them all up for a better view.

Adella gave Ariel a pretty blue starfish. "It always brings me luck," she told her sister.

King Triton placed a shiny pink pearl in Ariel's hand. "This belonged to your mother," he said. "She would have wanted you to have it."

Ariel's family helped her find something old, something new, something borrowed, and something blue for her wedding.

"You can borrow my favorite seashell hair clip to wear with your new gown," said her sister Aquata.

Ariel rushed to the beach to talk to her family. She asked her sisters to be her bridesmaids and Sebastian to be the ring bearer. Finally, she asked her father to give her away.

"It would be an honor," King Triton said.

Ariel went to Prince Eric with tears in her eyes. "I want a human wedding, but I want to share it with my family, too," she told him.

"Let's get married at sea on the royal ship," Eric suggested. "That way everyone can be there!"

After a busy day, Ariel went back to her room and thought about all the wonderful wedding plans. She wished her family could be there to celebrate her special day with her. But how? They all lived in the sea.

Next, Ariel visited Chef Louis. He promised to bake her the most scrumptious wedding cake ever! "I can't wait to taste it," Ariel said.

Carlotta worked for days making Ariel's dream
wedding gown. The princess had never seen anything like it.
"It's so beautiful!" cried Ariel.

Ariel knew Carlotta would be the best person to help with her dress.

"Is a human wedding gown hard to walk in?" she asked the maid.

Carlotta sketched some dress ideas for the bride-to-be. "Your gown will be made of the finest silks and satins," she told Ariel. "I promise you will be able to walk with no trouble at all."

Ariel had never been to a human wedding. Thankfully, she had a lot of people to help her prepare.

Grimsby, Eric's trusted servant, taught Ariel to dance on her two new legs. Before Ariel knew it, she was waltzing like a pro!

Princess Ariel and Prince Eric fell in love the first time they saw each other. Now, after a wild adventure, they were getting married!

Ariel's Royal Wedding

By Apple Jordan
Illustrated by the Disney Storybook Art Team
A Random House PICTUREBACK® Book

Random House New York

randomhouse.com/kids
ISBN 978-0-7364-3167-5
MANUFACTURED IN CHINA
10 9 8 7 6 5 4 3 2 1